ANGRY

BY SAVINA COLLINS

ILLUSTRATED BY
ANITA DUFALLA

Rourke
Educational Media
rourkeeducationalmedia.com

Scan for Related Titles
and Teacher Resources

Teaching Focus:
Concepts of Print: Ending Punctuation- Have students locate the ending punctuation for sentences in the book. Count how many times a period, question mark, or exclamation point is used. Which one is used the most? What is the purpose for each ending punctuation mark? Practice reading these sentences with appropriate expression.

Before Reading:

Building Academic Vocabulary and Background Knowledge
Before reading a book, it is important to set the stage for your child or student by using pre-reading strategies. This will help them develop their vocabulary, increase their reading comprehension, and make connections across the curriculum.
1. Read the title and look at the cover. *Let's make predictions about what this book will be about.*
2. Take a picture walk by talking about the pictures/photographs in the book. Implant the vocabulary as you take the picture walk. Be sure to talk about the text features such as headings, the Table of Contents, glossary, bolded words, captions, charts/diagrams, or index.
3. Have students read the first page of text with you then have students read the remaining text.
4. Strategy Talk – use to assist students while reading.
   - Get your mouth ready
   - Look at the picture
   - Think…does it make sense
   - Think…does it look right
   - Think…does it sound right
   - Chunk it – by looking for a part you know
5. Read it again.

Content Area Vocabulary
Use glossary words in a sentence.

angry
scream
stomp
together

After Reading:

Comprehension and Extension Activity
After reading the book, work on the following questions with your child or students in order to check their level of reading comprehension and content mastery.
1. *What happens when Iza's mom tells Iza no more cookies? (Summarize)*
2. *How does Iza deal with her anger? (Asking Questions)*
3. *What do you do when you become angry? (Text to self connection)*
4. *Do you think Iza will get angry again when her mom tells her she can't have another cookie? (Asking Questions)*

Extension Activity
Create an anger box. Find a shoe box and decorate it with tips on how to deal with anger. In your box put a favorite book, family photographs, and a journal to write in about your feelings.

TABLE OF CONTENTS

Cookies!.................................... 4

Angry 8

In My Room 16

Picture Glossary................... 23

About the Author 24

COOKIES!

I love cookies.

They are so yummy. I want another one!

Mom says, "No more cookies, Iza!"

Tears tickle my eyes.

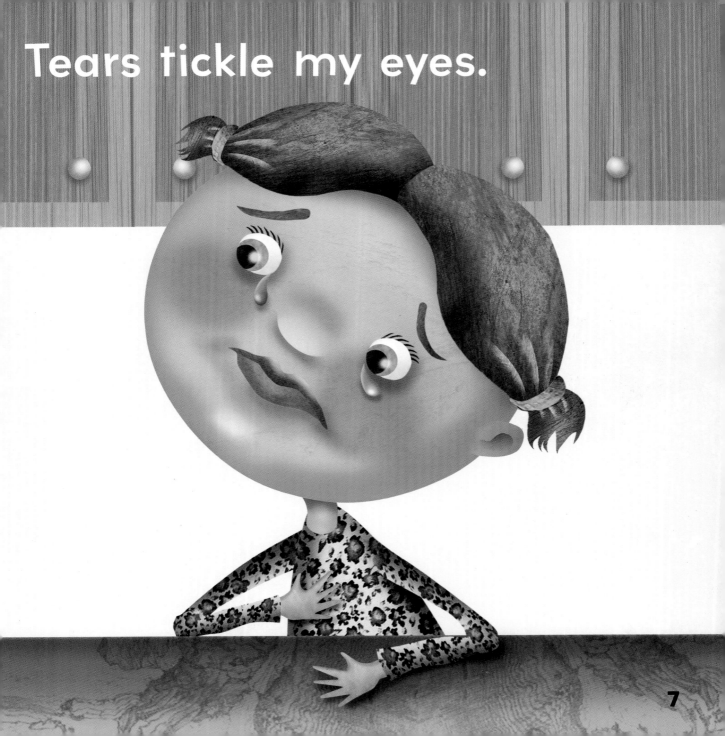

ANGRY
My heart beats fast.

My face feels hot.

I am **angry!**

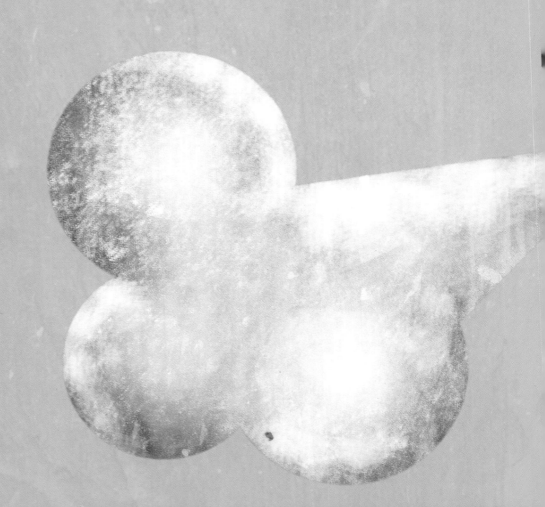

Maybe if I **stomp** my feet and **scream** I will get a cookie.

Mom says, "Go to your room, Iza."

I stomp my feet all the way to my room.

My anger makes me feel shaky inside.

IN MY ROOM
I take some deep breaths.

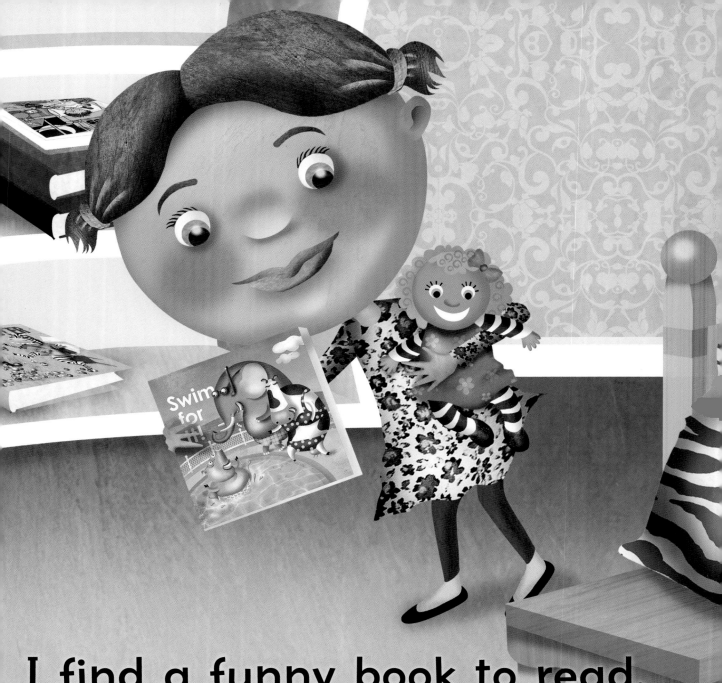

I find a funny book to read.

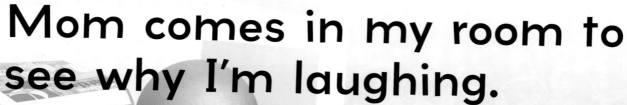

Mom comes in my room to see why I'm laughing.

We read **together.**

Mom puts her arms around me. She asks if I am still angry.

"Angry? What was I angry about?" I ask.

22

PICTURE GLOSSARY

 **angry** (ANG-gree): Feeling or showing annoyance or bad feelings toward someone or something.

 **scream** (skreem): To suddenly cry out in a loud and high voice.

 **stomp** (stahmp): To walk or move with very heavy or noisy steps.

 **together** (tuh-geTH-ur): Doing something with one another.

ABOUT THE AUTHOR

Savina Collins lives in Florida with her husband and 5 adventurous kids. She loves watching her kids surf at the beach. When she is not at the beach, Savina enjoys reading and taking long walks.

Meet The Author!
www.meetREMauthors.com

Library of Congress PCN Data

Angry/ Savina Collins
(I Have Feelings!)
ISBN 978-1-68342-141-2 (hard cover)
ISBN 978-1-68342-183-2 (soft cover)
ISBN 978-1-68342-214-3 (e-Book)
Library of Congress Control Number: 2016956523

Rourke Educational Media
Printed in the United States of America, North Mankato, Minnesota

www.rourkeeducationalmedia.com

Edited by: Keli Sipperley
Cover design and interior design by: Rhea Magaro-Wallace

Also Available as: